ABC HANUKKAH HUNT

For JBB, RBB, SMB, and JMB with love - T.B.

For all my wonderful family with lots of love - H.P.

KAR-BEN PUBLISHING, INC.
A division of Lerner Publishing Group, Inc.
241 First Avenue North
Minneapolis, MN 55401 U.S.A.
1-800-4-Karben

Website address: www.karben.com

Library of Congress Cataloging-in-Publication Data

Balsley, Tilda.
    ABC Hanukkah hunt / by Tilda Balsley ; illustrated by Helen Poole.
        p.   cm.
    Summary: Rhyming text reminds the reader of a significant word related to
Hanukkah for each letter of the alphabet.
    ISBN 978–1–4677–0420–5 (lib. bdg. : alk. paper)
    ISBN 978–1–4677–1637–6 (eBook)
    [1. Stories in rhyme. 2. Hanukkah—Fiction. 3. Alphabet.] I. Poole, Helen, ill.
II. Title.
PZ8.3.B2185Abc 2013
[E]—dc23   2012029187

Manufactured in the United States of America
1 – PC – 7/15/13

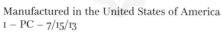

ABC HANUKKAH HUNT

by **Tilda Balsley**

Illustrated by **Helen Poole**

KAR-BEN
PUBLISHING

It's Hanukkah from **A** to **Z**.
An alphabet of things to see.

King **A**ntiochus! Where is he?

He would not let the Jews be free.

The leader's Judah. Can you find him?
Brave Maccabees all stand behind him.

Hunt for the **C**ruse of oil —it's small.

What miracle does it recall?

Freedom won, they celebrated.
See the temple **D**edicated.

So now we have **E**ight special days.
Special how? Describe the ways.

Which Menorah shows day three?
Count the **F**lames and you will see.

The **G**elt is in a golden pile.

Which winner has a chocolate smile?

Happy **H**anukkah! all around.
Can you find it upside down?

These artists have **I**magination.
Find the Hanukkah creation.

Where's **J**erusalem. A clue?

Look for the Holy Temple too.

KISLEV

SUNDAY	MONDAY	TUESDAY	WEDNESDAY	THURSDAY	FRIDAY	SATURDAY
1 KISLEV	2 KISLEV	3 KISLEV	4 KISLEV	5 KISLEV	6 KISLEV	7 KISLEV
8 KISLEV	9 KISLEV	10 KISLEV	11 KISLEV	12 KISLEV	13 KISLEV	14 KISLEV
15 KISLEV	16 KISLEV	17 KISLEV	18 KISLEV	19 KISLEV	20 KISLEV	21 KISLEV
22 KISLEV	23 KISLEV	24 KISLEV	25 KISLEV	26 KISLEV	27 KISLEV	28 KISLEV
29 KISLEV	30 KISLEV					

This calendar shows **K**islev's here.

Which holiday starts this time of year?

Who's frying **L**atkes in the pan?

And who's the biggest latke fan?

Different kinds and colors, too.
Which **M**enorah's right for you?

Nun, Gimmel, Hey, Shin.

Find the dreidels we can spin.

Sufganiyot! This **O**ne's for me.

How many doughnuts do you see?

A time for giving to each other.
Which **P**resent is for little brother?

Be **Q**uick, be quick, they're at the door.
More guests are here. How many more?

This family's **R**eading—take a look.
Can you find the Hanukkah book?

What does a **S**hamash candle do?

Look at Dad, he's showing you.

A **T**zedakah box—what goes inside?

Who needs your help? You can decide.

The family's gathered around to eat—
but look who's taken **U**ncle's seat?

All **V**oices sing a Hanukkah song.

What family member "howls" along?

Which **W**indows shine with candles bright, sharing Hanukkah tonight?

E**X**tra dishes in the sink.

Who's the biggest help, do you think?

Next Year is Hanukkah again.

Which pictures show what you'll do then?

"Sweet dreams of Hanukkah," Mom said.

Is everybody tucked in bed?

ABOUT HANUKKAH

Hanukkah is an eight-day Festival of Lights that celebrates the victory of the Maccabees over the mighty armies of Syrian King Antiochus. According to legend, when the Maccabees came to restore the Holy Temple in Jerusalem, they found one jug of pure oil, enough to keep the menorah burning for just one day. But a miracle happened, and the oil burned for eight days. On each night of the holiday, we add an additional candle to the *menorah* until there are eight candles plus the *shamash*, the "helper" candle. We exchange gifts, play the game of *dreidel*, and eat *latkes* (potato pancakes) and *sufganiyot* (jelly donuts) fried in oil to remember this victory for religious freedom.

ABOUT THE AUTHOR

Tilda Balsley is the author of many children's books, including *Let My People Go!*, *The Queen Who Saved Her People*, *Maccabee!*, *Oh No, Jonah!* and four Jewish-themed Sesame Street titles about Grover, Big Bird and friends. She lives with her husband and their rescue Shih Tzu in Reidsville, NC.

ABOUT THE ILLUSTRATOR

Helen Poole graduated with a B.A. in Illustration from the University of Central Lancashire, where she discovered working digitally and never looked back! Her first "commission" came at age 11 when she fractured her fingers (thankfully not ones on her drawing hand!) and was asked to do some illustrations of cartoon characters in various states of injury for her local hospital. She loves to drink herbal tea and sing loudly along to her eclectic music collection as she works.